W9-ATK-449

The Gryphon Press

—a voice for the voiceless—

This book is dedicated, with sincere gratitude,
to each person who rescues, fosters, adopts, and takes responsible care of an animal.

I wish to honor in particular the incredible Sarah Kent Eckhoff,
rescuer of animals and people,
whose gentle care and vision changed lives. —C. B.

To all the four-foots, whose wisdom resides inside us all,
just waiting to be put to use. —A. H.

Sit! Stay! Read! Series

Copyright © 2007 text by Claire Buchwald
Copyright © 2007 art by Amelia Hansen
All rights reserved. This book, or parts thereof,
may not be reproduced without permission from the publisher,
The Gryphon Press, 6808 Margaret's Lane, Edina, MN 55439.

Reg. U.S. Patent. & Tm Office. The scanning, uploading and distribution
of this book via the Internet or via any other means without the permission
of the publisher is illegal and punishable by law. Please purchase only authorized
electronic editions, and do not participate in or encourage electronic piracy of copyrighted
materials. Your support of the author's and artist's rights is appreciated.

Text design by Connie Kuhnz
Text set in Galliard by BookMobile
Printed in Canada by Friesens Corporation

Library of Congress Control Number: 2009904014

ISBN: 978-0940719-08-8

3 5 7 9 10 8 6 4

A portion of profits from this book will be
donated to shelters and animal rescue societies.

I am the voice of the voiceless:
Through me, the dumb shall speak;
Till the deaf world's ear be made to hear
The cry of the wordless weak.

—from a poem by Ella Wheeler Wilcox, early 20th-century poet

Are You Ready for Me?

Written by Claire Buchwald
Illustrated by Amelia Hansen

You want a puppy or dog. Maybe it will be me.
If you choose me, I will love and trust you.

I will be your friend. I will also need you.
What will your life be like if you decide to take me home?

It is a lot of work to take care of a dog, especially a puppy.
You will need to keep me clean
and clip my nails when they get too long.

I should be brushed as often as I need to be, at least once a week,
and when my coat has burrs in it.

I should be fed wholesome food at least once a day.
Don't forget to wash out my bowl and keep it clean.

Just as you have to drink when you are thirsty,
I must have fresh water all the time.

I can't use the toilet like you—
and sometimes I just can't wait until you walk me outside.
If your family can put in a doggy door that goes out to a fenced yard,
I will be able to go outside when I need to.

Until you know that I am house-trained,
be patient with me while I learn to go outdoors.
I will still have accidents.
Remember that you make mistakes too.

It is not fair to me to keep me tied up, chained in the yard,
or locked away in a cage for many hours.
Like all dogs, I need space and freedom.
But I am happiest when I am close to you.

I need your attention.
Every day you should spend time with me, petting me.
This is time when you focus on me. We can also cuddle
when you sleep, read, watch television, or talk on the phone.

I have a lot of energy! Every day we should play outside for *at least* 20 minutes. Think of it as doggy recess. Take me outside to your yard, or to a dog park, where we can run, play ball or Frisbee, and maybe romp with other dogs.

I need two long walks a day—
even if it is cold or raining.
Don't forget to bring a bag to clean up my poop!

Please be fair. Don't be angry when I chew your stuff.
Give me my own toys, safe things to chew.
Chewing, sniffing, digging, and barking—these are things that dogs do.
Teach me when and where I can do these dog things.

You are my protector.
You are the one who cares most about me.
Don't ever let anyone hurt me or tease me.

Your voice is the most important sound in the world to me.
I especially need to hear you say, "Good dog!"

Remember to greet me, let me out, and walk me every day after school—
before you play, watch TV, or go out with your friends.

Just as you go to the doctor for checkups and when you are sick,

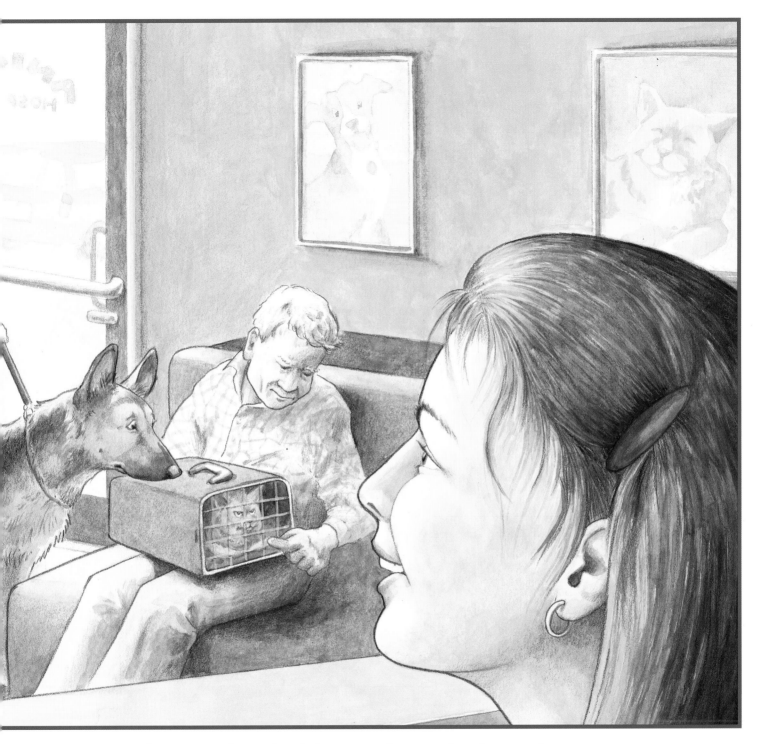

I need to go to the animal doctor—the veterinarian—at least once a year
and when I am not feeling well.

Your mom and dad take care of you, no matter what.
Now that you know what you will need to do to take good care of me,

can you promise that day after day, year after year,
no matter how busy you are, you will take care of me as if I were your child?

If you do not think that you or your family can do all of these things, that's okay,
but you should not get a dog now. Maybe you can get one when you are older.
You can still love dogs. You can still have dog friends. You can walk a neighbor's dog.
I will always remember what a grown-up decision you made not to get a dog now.

If you and your parents are sure
that you can and will take care of a dog like me
for my whole life, then you are ready to have a dog.
Let's go home!

If you and your parents are sure
that you can and will take care of a puppy like me
for my whole life, then you are ready to have a puppy.
I hope it will be me!

CONTRACT

We, the _____ family, do solemnly promise that:

WE KNOW:

____ we have the space for a dog.

____ we have the time for a dog.

____ we have the patience for a dog.

____ we have the money to feed and care for a dog.

____ we are not allergic to dogs.

____ we are allowed to have dogs where we live.

____ we can stay in a place where dogs are allowed.

____ we can love a dog and be good caregivers.

____ we will not get tired of a dog.

____ a dog is not a thing—it is a living part of our family.

WE WILL NEVER:

____ abandon our dog.

____ hurt or tease our dog.

____ sell or give our dog to someone who would hurt him/her.

____ let our dog run free in the neighborhood or by streets.

____ punish our dog for something she/he cannot help.

____ ignore our dog.

____ have our dog without a safe collar and ID tag.

____ leave our dog alone all day in a crate.

____ tie our dog outside for hours on end.

____ leave our dog outside without shelter or shade.

WE WILL:

____ give our dog high-quality food and clean his/her dish regularly.

____ make sure our dog has access to fresh water all the time.

____ spay or neuter our dog.

____ license our dog.

____ provide a dry, clean place for our dog to live.

____ give our dog regular medical attention from a veterinarian.

____ make sure our dog gets his/her shots.

____ keep our dog safe and off the street.

____ walk our dog at least twice a day.

____ train our dog to be well-mannered around people and other dogs.

____ play with our dog daily, ideally at the same regular times, because dogs need routines.

____ pet our dog every day.

____ talk to our dog every day.

____ groom our dog regularly, bathe him/her, and clip his/her nails when necessary.

____ spend at least some time home with our dog every day (or have somebody else be there with our dog).

____ love and care for our dog even when he/she is old.

____ provide safe play and chew toys.

We make all these promises. We promise to love our dog and care for him/her as a member of our family.

Signed, _____

(sign and date)

 If you cannot put a check mark next to all of the answers, you are not ready to own a dog at this time. Until you are, you can help dogs and other animals, volunteer your time, or have a pet that takes less time and expense.

Go to the Gryphon Press website, www.thegryphonpress.com, to download the complete *Are You Ready for Me?* kit, with a We Are Ready for a Dog contract you can print out, as well as an award certificate for the child who decides *not* to get a dog at this time.